MW00827805

OH BABY

OH BABY

Flash Fictions and Prose Poems
by Kim Chinquee

RAVENNA PRESS
2008

Ravenna Press books are listed at Bowker Books in Print
and are available to the trade through our primary distributor,
AtlasBooks, a division of BookMasters:
http://www.bookmasters.com/atlasdistribution/index.html.
For personal orders or other information, contact the editor at
http://www.ravennapress.com/books
or write to Ravenna Press
2910 E. 57th Ave., Ste. 10B-310
Spokane, WA 99223

ISBN: 978-0-9791921-8-0
LCCN: 2008920241

Cover Design: Pier Rodelon

ACKNOWLEDGMENTS

Most of these works have been previously published, many in an earlier form, some with alternate titles. Grateful acknowledgment to the editors of *Anemone Sidecar, The Avatar Review, Caketrain, Conjunctions, Denver Quarterly, elimae, Fiction International, Ghoti, In Posse Review, Konundrum Engine Literary Review, Memorious, Mississippi Review, Moonshinestill, Noon, Opium Magazine, Phan-tasmagoria, Pindeldyboz, Phoebe, Quick Fiction, Redivider, Salome, [sic], Sidebrow, Sleepingfish, So to Speak, Spork,* and *3am Magazine.*

Also special thanks to my mentors and teachers—Frederick Barthelme, Steven Barthelme, Richard Powers, Mary Robison, Jean Thompson, Diane Williams and Tom Williams—and to my editors—Cooper Renner and Kathryn Rantala. And I must not forget Francis Ford Coppola (for Zoetrope) and the Hot Pants writing group.

To my son Josh

CONTENTS

OH BABY

Batter

I washed my grandma's chickens, soaking bodies, stripping feathers, headless. Kool-Aid made me hiccup. My father yelled shutthefuckup. I pretended. My mouth was taped with duct tape. I caused my father's ulcers. I was about to bat. The coach said I was bunting. I knew how. I was fast.

Bluebell

A backwash of people stood looking at the geyser at the mall.

"It's so fake," she said.

"A micron, a disaster," said her friend.

They went to The Gap and tried on pastel T-shirts.

"We look like shit," the first one said.

"Like cowpox," said the second.

They put back on their street clothes. They wore jean jackets and Capri pants, frizzy hairdos with expensive highlights. They were twins. They passed the new geyser, laughing at a screaming baby with ribbons in her pigtails.

They said that never, in a million years, would they ever have a baby. They went to Hot Topic, where they bought leather bracelets, clothes with chains and shirts with slogans on them. They hid things in their pockets. They could spend millions.

They Went to a Place

He shrugged and sipped his water. When the waiter brought shrimp cocktail, they each picked a creature and dipped it in sauce, then left the tails. "It's not bad," he said. The mother looked at her child for once. They shared a glass of wine, the boy sipping when the waiter wasn't looking. She left a big tip and in the lot the boy started the car. He drove. She made sure he stopped thoroughly.

Cuppa Tea

She lifted cup from saucer, talking about porterhouse dreams. Her friend waved to someone with a June-is-Dairy-Month T-shirt, got up; they hugged. The drink was off on something. The friend sat again, said sorry it was a while. Then, so the dream? Tea woman looked up like huh?

Look What Sue Can Do

An announcer dangled fish and sang, "Look what Sue can do!" Dolphins jumped and twisted.

She came here for a conference. Timmy laughed as a dolphin wagged and squirmed, dancing. She watched it soar above the water. Everyone was clapping.

"That was nice," the ex-husband said, after it was over. His face was dripping. His hairline was receding. There were lines around his eyes. This was the man she ran from. He was that man who slammed her.

Timmy got a towel and gave it to his father. They dried themselves and they put on hats. "What next?" the ex-husband said.

She would go back to the hotel. She did not come to visit her ex-husband. The men would go to the arcade. They would play and shoot the baskets. She looked back. They were far gone, heading in their own direction.

January Usual

After the fourth glass of Merlot, she told him it was over. She was sure of it, there at Motel 6. It was 30-degrees, oddly warm. In Chicago, they'd slept at the Hilton. They'd walked down Michigan, holding hands and watching mimes. Now, at Motel 6 he woke her, packing, saying he had to fix his heater. She told him she was sorry. He said he knew. She said, no, I'm really sorry. She said that a lot. He brushed her cheek, looked at her, said, Honey. He put their bags in his trunk. She got in the passengers', and he drove them back to his house where they waited for the repairman.

Needlestick

She sat in the ER, waiting for gamma-globulin. Her shift was over. She wore blue scrubs.

It wasn't like she'd imagined, first practicing on a peach or a tomato. Her first time was in her classmate, his arm; he was big and blue-eyed, an airman from Chicago. She had to move the needle around to find the vein and he got sweaty, then fainted.

Today she'd drawn an elderly veteran wearing a ponytail, bandana. She'd been at it three years. Needle in, this guy had a seizure. While trying to control him, she let go of the needle, which fell out of him and poked her. She was sure he was positive.

Grace

Our roads intersected, though we didn't live close. She lived on Harold Road, which was her last name, the road named after her ancestors, and I lived on Strauperstein, my surname.

She had a swing set and a pool. She even had a fawn in a cage in the barn that used to house bulls. I had an older sister. She had a younger one who died when she was four of a heart condition. I remember the funeral, watching my mom quiver.

She got a horse that year, and one day she saddled it and told me to get on. I'd never been on a horse before except at the fair, for ten cents a ride. I didn't remember it really, but there was a picture.

I wanted her to like me. I got on and she nudged the horse. His name was Vent. He took off and I bumped and bumped and he went faster. We were in her grandpa's hay field. I tried holding on and then fell off, landing on my shoulder.

Vent ran and it took two days to find him. She'd never even been on the horse herself. The next week, her dad sold the horse at somebody's auction.

When my cast came off, I had to make a fist to make my muscles stronger. At her place, she took me to the barn where the fawn used to be. She said she had to show me something and told me to get in the pen. I felt brave. She smiled at me. I saw a bull come charging, pumping his legs. I ran and jumped the fence. She laughed. Her lips were dark and her teeth were white.

Slot Machine

She watches rolls falling, at a man who looks like a potato. Her stepfather used to come here. He died. He spent millions. There's oxygen and dinging. She gets behind the wheel of a very nice car.

We Were Ready for a Ballroom

Sometimes after church on Sundays, we would drive an hour into town, where we would find McDonald's, and my dad would order groups of fries and burgers, and we would grab what we wanted from the tray. My sister liked picking off her cheese, and my mom preferred a lot of catsup, dipping what she'd eat into a little saucer, and my dad loved everything, it seemed, devouring as if he were somebody homeless. I picked off my bun, only eating that and watching mostly, sipping on my Diet Coca-Cola. Nobody said a thing, and I would stare at the statue of Ronald in his hat and his big shoes, pretending we were ready for a ballroom. On the way back home, my dad would burp, putting on his blinker. When I looked over at my sister, we'd smile. After we got home and we knew our dad was in the barnyard, my sister and I would jump into our bed, crawling under covers. We talked nonstop, holding each other until suppertime.

Like a House

She'd been up all night, walking loops around the flightline, trying to waste her energy on something. She'd gone out barefoot, her dog Buster on the leash. It was eighty-degree weather, humid, and they sat next to the bay and bugs bit at her ankles. She didn't want to go home. She didn't want to go and find her husband absent--that was why she left in the first place--it had been two a.m. and where was he? It was nothing unusual.

She'd worked all day, poking patients with needles, her belly sticking out, the baby doing tricks inside her tummy. Her feet were swollen, her body constantly hungry, so she kept a stash of butterscotch candy in her pocket, always sucking. Her co-workers said to her in passing, "How much longer?" and "You're like a house!"

But now she thought about the night, about the darkness and the lights and the airfield. No planes were flying in. Everything was calm and it was pretty. The colored lights glowed like a present. Her baby kicked and she started crying.

It was four a.m. She didn't know what would wait at home, but she had to be at work at six for rounds. She thought maybe she felt a contraction, so she took a little puff. She would stay there until the feeling went away. She'd stay there as long as she needed. Buster ran in circles. He was barking. She told him it was too early. It was too early, she said. It was too early for anything.

History

The place was Southern England, with green and sheep and rabbits. The base wasn't big in size, but it was worthy and important, in World War II and history. And then there was Desert Storm, but Desert Storm was over.

I was twenty-two. After I arrived and started to unpack and my son started to explore the empty drawers, I gave him a bottle and retired to bed. I awoke to knocking on the door, reminded, and answered to a pumpkin and another kid in a Dalmatian costume. "Trick or treat!" they said, singing.

There were just five of us: the physician, the desk clerk, and two perverts, male nurse aides, and then me, the lab technician. I ordered equipment, supplies, set up quality control. Took down Desert Storm leftovers. When the people left before, they left hard, and now junk was everywhere.

My husband was a lab tech just like me. He was at that base for Desert Storm while I collected blood in Mississippi; when he came home, he came back different, which made me wish he'd stay gone. He acted surprised when I got orders. I ditched him and took my orders. I flew a C5 over, trying to shush my son with suffocating hugs, wax earplugs and a bottle.

I heard stuff, found stuff, ran into women on base

and I wondered how he knew them. They laughed and giggled, wearing no bras and thin shirts. I tried to concentrate on work and on my baby. When my boy laughed, he laughed like his father. At work, I found old charts with his initials: documentations, daily checks, temperatures and values.

Now everyone was sick. It was sinuses and viruses. When I didn't have lab work, I checked in patients. I penetrated people's histories. People will tell you anything.

I soaked up every detail. After we closed up, I went to the bunker and dusted out the cobwebs. I unfolded an old wheelchair, hearing it creak. I didn't smoke, but found an old pack of Camels and sat on the chair and lit up, thinking of my husband's old butts. I put the smoke out in a plastic spit tray.

Knocked Over

I was about to lose my job and then a lawsuit and my kid was hooked on sniffing. I felt like someone else, like I was knocked over or about to lose a fight or maybe in the middle of a marathon when you hit the halfway mark and the people who signed up for the half can quit, but if you were dumb enough to sign up for the whole and didn't go on then you were still a loser. But I still had strength enough to know I was okay, and I felt nothing mattered although in a hopeful way, because before this mess I felt hopeless, but now I felt dumb for having felt that.

I took Shark for a jog, pulling the leash. He had a fancy collar. He was the biggest dog I'd had and I grew up on a farm with enough dogs to last a lifetime. He had a heavy coat that he liked to launder up with dirt and I imagined his coat infested with people's problems. Sometimes I dreamt of secrets, ghosts under his fur. He was smarter than my last dog Muffin, who perished in my father's barn after it caught fire.

Shark made tracks in the snow and the world moved around me: people walking, some in hats and scarves and mittens, hot breaths pushing into cold air. Cars passed each other, honking. Shark ran with me. He started running faster, so I released him, watching him head.

Knick-Knack

We sat on Jesus statues, holding Bibles, names engraved. My mother said to pick a souvenir, so I picked a knick-knack angel with a tilted head. The angel held a harp and her right cheek held a teardrop. Later we went to a park where deer got close, eating from our hands, stepping on our sandals. We took a ride to the Dells. My mom said, Elvis died. She'd heard it on the radio. She cried real hard. I didn't know who Elvis was and neither did my sister. We went home early, to our little castle, and during the ride, my mom said it would be good if I collected angels. When we got back, my dad found cockroaches and went a little crazy. He ran around saying cockroachcockroachcockroach. He said it all the way to the hospital.

Doing It Over

She tells me her new guy fixed her house that got damaged from Katrina. She says he lives in our old parts and we start talking Midwestern. We say Packers PackersPackersPackers! Emphasizing the aaaaa, and then a new word, the eeeeeee and longation of the rrr, saying beeeerrrr. We do it over and over, over. She mentions him again, the new one. He loves the Packers and I think of all the Packer stories—another long and distant friend, high school friends fucking and falling, fucking and falling, fucking married Packers.

She says this new guy can help. She says it's, like, been centuries.

Cook

My mother baked things. Always. One time, she made brownies, saying they were for our retriever, Savage. "It's his prize," she said. She knew I wouldn't eat them. She told me to take a nap. When I woke up the brownies were all gone and so was my mother. She was lying on a sofa. She smelled like gasoline.

Game

By noon, the ballgame was over. Todd and I rode our bikes past a field with tall and wilting weeds. He looked back. I was behind him, smelling the lilacs from the distance. He told me not to hurry. I was Sunflower Wagner. I was a woman. I was twenty. He won. I was in the stands. He hit three home runs. He had a wicked punch. We rode by the cemetery. Someone was lowering a coffin.

Eve

It is fifteen below so we stay inside, making candy out of pudding that we put in the freezer. We recycle melted chocolate. It is a reunion of sorts.

Tenant

She took a chair to the curb. The boys sharing her driveway looked eighteen. They were maybe in a band, flapping their guitars, crucifying strangers. Their skin was waxy. "Want some chairs?" she said. The blond came first. "I have tons," she said. She pointed while they lifted for more.

Strings

I heard things from my son's room. I thought horrible things. "What's wrong?" I said. "What is it?" I touched his hair, which he'd bleached to dye it blue, only the blue had faded. Tears ran from the tilted angles of his eyes, dripping to his ears. He cried harder. He sounded like a man.

Identical

They ate their steak and bought candy bars for the ride. They fell asleep on the bus, relieved to be away from the technical instructors, who yelled at them for not folding in perfect angles. The twins leaned into each other.

Stall

We started stealing her dad's beer, sharing the bottle in a corner of the hayloft. She would hiccup and I would plug my mouth. "My dad's a dickhead," she said once. I had no idea what a dickhead might be. We wandered and found a bull. It had big horns.

Sunrise

She placed her foot in a pail full of worms to accelerate her healing. Her son had fetched them early, put them in his bucket.

They sat in the back yard, the mother drinking Kool-Aid spiked with vodka, the boy with his juice.

"Mom," he said. "When can we go fishing?"

"Maybe when my bloody foot heals," she said, and took another sip. She put a hand on his head, the other holding up the glass that made the ice clink. She sipped long and good and hard, almost with feeling.

Pump

At the pump, she bickered over prices. Her baby sucked, all buckled.

She went and paid, thinking of how it could be simpler. Her card had hit the max.

Lumps had thickened in her skin, which she figured she deserved. She had thought she could finally buy better things.

She got back to the car. How dumb was it to leave your baby? The baby was still sucking, tucked.

She drove a long way.

Rounds

She watched the bevel of the needle move into her hand. It was her control. She'd been drawing his blood daily, waking him early, breaking up his sleep. He'd say, "Hello, my little angel," and she'd see the saliva that had dried up on his chin, smell his ill and sleeping scent. One morning, she awoke him, but he wasn't speaking. She took his blood, then punctured her thumb on the recap.

Our Fathers

When we were in church, my father yelled in the middle of the sermon, "God help me, help me, help me. Our Father Who Art in Heaven, God help me, help me, help me."

Viral

This town was flat with lots of cornfields and now I lived states away. My ex sat opposite me, lounging on the sofa. I sat on a chair, and my son slept on the bed with IVs dripping, medication.

I'd only seen my ex one other time since the divorce eleven years before. He flew in that morning. My son had always lived with me.

"Where's Festopolis?" he said.

I said, "His name is Leonidas."

My son turned over in his sleep, cried. He was almost an adult.

I got up and felt his forehead. "He's roasting," I said, and I remembered the days of infanthood.

"He'll survive," my ex said. "The doc said it was viral."

I ran my hands over my son's forehead, put a cold cloth on his neck, but it startled him and he woke. "You have a fever," I told him, and he looked at me with eyes that seemed drunk.

"So when you and Aristotle getting married?" my ex said.

He got out his laptop and showed me pictures of his newborn. "She's on maternity," he said. "This kid's big."

I closed my eyes and thought about my boyfriend.

I'd moved two years before and we did everything long distance. Now he was away, visiting his country.

"You need anything?" my ex said. He spoke of sobriety and money. He said, "You okay with things?"

I opened my eyes and looked at him. There was a lot that I could tell him. I never asked for more.

He threw me his wallet. "Take what you need," he said. I told him that was a stupid idea and threw it back.

He pulled out some dollars, leaving a stack on the table. Then he left, saying he was hungry.

"Aren't you?" he said.

Toy

"I have to practice," he said.

He was always saying that. It was something she was used to. She'd given many times, just waiting. He was more successful, a musician.

Evenings, he taught her how to cook. He made his favorite, eggplant, steamed with fresh tomato. She chewed; he was pouring from the kettle, describing ingredients, the spices. He would have to tell her more than once for her to remember.

She tried to paint the kettle, but it did not represent her visions: the way it tasted to her starving palate. He would cover leftovers with foil, and she would paint the foil, and put the painting in a binder.

At night, there would be fog. When she would visit, they would go for walks, sifting through the park. Then they would go upstairs, to his exotic bedroom.

It was almost Spring. This seemed like something different. He could teach her something. For now, she was happy just to give. Once, she told him that, and he kept on calling her his sweetheart. He said she was really something.

Tracks

One day, the trains stopped, but her stories went on, went on, becoming more haunting and disastrous, faster in their tracks. I tried to fool her, making the choo and drum of slow trains passing. At first she went along, but I knew she was smart, and I had to work harder at deceiving. I tried finding ways of making the sounds more real, would spend my nights at home, making songs on my recorder.

One day, she hugged me first, then hit me. I took all of my devices, walking to the tracks. I played my stuff and waited.

King and Queen

She's been soliciting rich prospective clients, sending envelopes with letters that read, "I'd love to sell a house!" She's only had one sale, a condo to a cousin. She's been reading birth announcements in the Life section, parents needing more room.

"Play with me," her daughter says.

She thinks about the envelopes waiting in her office. She wants to buy expensive groceries: mangos, organic lettuce, vegan bread. Her daughter likes hamburgers, French fries and, lately, sandwiches from Subway. Lately Frida has been making Ramen Noodles. Eggs and toast and macaroni.

Her daughter talks about each piece: the king and queen, the knight, the rook, the bishop and the pawn, telling her mother of their power. She eats. Her daughter says she wants some. Button paws the hem of the red-and-yellow curtain.

"What kinds of houses do you sell?" her daughter says.

She tells her daughter, "Shhh." She looks for a Stalemate.

Shoe

Somebody's sneaker was flattened on the highway. She saw it, running by on gravel. Her shoes were clean, yet worn.

Cars passed, but she ignored them.

She was high from endorphins. She thought about last weekend. They had all been out together: her two lovers, who were also her two boyfriends. She'd been drinking gin and tonics. When she woke in the morning, she didn't remember. She was bruised and aching. She called one boyfriend, then the other. She felt awful and hung over. She told them this. One, and then the other. One boyfriend told her she was fine. The other said that they were alcoholics. She thought about the two of them. One, and then the other. She'd told each of them she loved them. They'd been the best of friends ever since she could remember.

The next day, she went running. She'd always been a runner. But not with her two boyfriends, who were also her two lovers. With them, she had forgotten. So she made a rigid schedule. She'd go for miles. She'd be running for forever.

Now her pores were purging sweat. She was like an ice cube, melting from inside.

She thought about the flattened shoe, wondering who it might belong to. It was without a partner. It was not a pair.

Sandpaper

Going out for pancakes, he drove through the construction.

She was numb from exhaustion.

She'd been looking through a peephole. He'd told her from the start he didn't believe in anything long distance. They both knew she would be leaving.

She spoke of her determination. He didn't trust himself, he'd said, he needed someone there to touch him, hold him, feel him. Someone there to hear him.

He'd told her all along, over the whole time that she'd known him. And on their vacation, stepping through the sea, he told her that he loved her.

Now they were together on his carpet. She was weeping. He said to her, "What were you expecting?"

Oh Baby

I took a jog, pushing on the stroller. My baby screamed, so I hushed him with a bottle. It was up and down, around, and fields were gold. Old buildings of stone reminded me of movies. Sheep baahed and I baahed back, pushing on the jogger. I was new to divorce. I could run far. I'd gone miles, finding Bourton-on-the-Water. I saw paved sidewalks, pubs. My baby woke, throwing out his bottle. Something banged. Things fell from the sky and he laughed.

Olives and Fruit

They were on the twenty-second floor. She heard far-off music, got out of bed and looked out the window, down. She put in her contacts, then looked out again, seeing tiny figures on the road: splotches of people in colors, a moving kaleidoscope. Heads were like bottle caps. "Looks like a race," she said. "Everybody's walking."

She got back into bed, next to his warm body, his arms pulling her in.

They reunited yesterday, him driving two hours his way; she drove four. They were professors at different universities. He was a musician. She taught art.

She touched his chest, fingering his hair. She kissed his shoulder.

"I dreamt of this woman and my child," he said.

In her dream, she played a blue piano, but the legs kept breaking, then later there were three dogs. One died, the others ran around. And there was a baby wrapped in plastic wrap, its mouth stuffed. She held the baby.

She said, "Maybe you should meet him."

At breakfast people wore T-shirts in memory of loved ones. Some wore suits and dresses. He wore the jacket she'd given him for his birthday; she had on a silky shirt with the one-hundred-dollar pants she bought the last time in Chicago. The waiter poured water, and said, If you're a mother, Happy Mother's Day. She tried to think of what to order. She heard people talking at the next table about cancer and the walk, and she longed for her stepfather. The Cancer Walk was over. Her son was home. She'd have to call her mother. She'd get the continental. He ordered the American, and the waiter gave them coffee.

"Is there Mother's Day in Cyprus?" she asked.

He talked about his relatives in Cyprus, who prepared their own grains, olives, and grew fruit. He'd last seen them at his father's funeral. He'd gotten the news of his father's death one night after she arrived. She'd stayed up with him as he grieved, pouring himself whiskey, and the next day, she took him to the airport.

She ate her muffin and banana and he ate his eggs and bacon. When they weren't eating, they were touching: hand-on-knee, hand-in-hand or hand-on-arm, resting on the table.

Now he talked about his cousins, who lived on the streets in Nicosia, raising and butchering chickens, selling eggs to people like his mother.

"My grandmother raised chickens," she said. "She butchered them." She thought of her grandmother's red bandana, her leaning over a stump, ax ready.

For dessert, they shared a bowl of oatmeal. He said he better call his mother, then reviewed a conversation he'd had with his mother the week before, when he finally told his mom he had a son. He said he resented his son's mother, who'd sent him a letter saying she needed more support.

"If she makes things difficult," he said. "My son will never see his father."

The woman listened, feeding herself oatmeal. It was warm in her mouth.

§

Back in their room, he unbuttoned his shirt. It was his signal. She put her jewelry on the dresser, and he lay on the bed, patting the spot next to him. She got on the bed, beside.

Afterwards, he called out to her, "I love you," then he sort of trembled, saying, "You're really wonderful. I love you so much."

§

At check-out, the hotel clerk asked if he was Greek. The clerk spoke to him in Greek—she was chubby with dark hair, and the woman wondered if the mother of his child looked anything like her. He'd said she was Greek, that she got pregnant for one reason.

She listened to the clerk. She tried to understand the language.

They put their bags in their respective cars, leaving them in the lot. They walked down Balbo, to Michigan, and she saw remnants of the Walk: more people in their matching t-shirts and different numbers, some people with balloons, and tents were set up along the park, lines of port-a-potties. She had flashbacks of the marathon she'd run there, in Chicago.

"Reminds me of the marathon," she said.

"The time," he said, "you got drunk the night before?"

She remembered dry heaving at the end, leaning over the bridge they were now passing over. She'd gotten a taxi, the driver weaving in and out of traffic while she hung her head out the window.

They walked past cones that people were beginning to pick up, past the crew with t-shirts that read Volunteer, and past an ambulance that was parked in a clearing. "A woman died," she said, "at that race."

They crossed the street. "She just collapsed and

died. She was in her thirties."

They went toward the lake. "I could have died," she said. She remembered her running buddy Larry, meeting him in the hotel room. Larry used to be her friend. He was fast. He finished in under three hours. She told Larry pre-race night that she'd sleep on the floor, but he said if she slept in the bed, he wouldn't touch her. She woke to his hand on her breast, and she moved to the floor. She was always slower, never winning.

"It was my last race," she said. She told him about her hopes to run the Boston, a qualifying time. She started out too fast and lost her breath, her energy, dry-heaving her way through it.

They walked along the lakeshore, and inside her head, she tried to retrace. She been to Chicago since the marathon, but now, staying at the Hilton, seeing the fervor of the people made her feel nostalgic. Her son had been with her mother for that marathon weekend, and he would have been eight or nine or ten then. Now he was sixteen. It was Mother's Day. She had to call her mother. Her boyfriend didn't want children. They'd been together two years and she knew what to give him. She massaged his hands. They were made for the piano.

They headed to Navy Pier and she told him that this walk reminded her of San Diego, where she'd gone to a conference and had an interview. It was the busy-ness, the water. It was right before she'd met him. She got the job.

"I can't believe the weather," he said. Yesterday they needed hats and scarves and mittens, and today people ran in shorts and tank tops, a pair of bicyclists with bare chests. Dogs were pulled on leashes, babies sucked on bottles in their strollers. An elderly couple walked by in matching purple glasses.

He asked if he should get a lawyer.

"It wouldn't hurt," she said. She'd told him of her

situation. It was long over.

He was quiet for a minute. Someone screamed from far away, and the sun hid behind clouds. She reminded him she'd been getting child support through the state of North Dakota. She said, "It's better when it's over."

"I'm not sacrificing," he said.

She said it's hard alone. She pulled him closer, arms around. They always stayed close, arm-in-arm, hand-in-hand, hips against another's.

As they wound around the lake, they got to Navy Pier, where boats were loading, people passed, and everything was color. The shops and restaurants reminded her of somewhere fake like Disney, and she figured everything was probably real expensive. She said she'd never been to Navy Pier.

"I took you here," he said.

She tried finding anything familiar. Nothing seemed real. She looked around, trying to convince herself she'd been there. They stopped and she paid five bucks for lemonade, then had to use the bathroom, so they walked faster. Maybe he had another girlfriend. There'd been other girlfriends with her husband. She wasn't married anymore. Neither of them was.

They walked to the end, leaned over the rail, and looked down into the water. She put her face up to his cheek. And then her phone rang. It was her son. "Hi," she said. He was coughing. "Are you ok?" she said.

They went back, retracing, and when they reached a statue of a sitting man, she remembered some other time, seeing people talking to the sculpture. "Ok," she said to him. "I remember. I recall that man." It was all she could remember. It's hard to tell what's real.

As they walked, they continued talking. Under the viaducts, birds flew before their faces, the wind blew a bit, and people passed them like before.

He said he wished they lived closer. She thought of them together in a high rise, cooking rice with mussels. They'd sip Sauvignon Blanc, Pinot Grigio, Merlot. They'd feed each other berries at sunrise, truffles when it set. Afternoons he'd compose at his piano while she painted. Their sons might even be together.

"I miss you," he said. Birds flew all around them.

"You need to see your son," she said. "You do."

He talked of moving back to Cyprus and staying there forever.

She called her own child on her cell phone. He said he'd taken Tylenol. He asked when she'd be home.

She took her boyfriend's hand. He said, "You better go."

She'd been without him for a very long time. "I know," she said. "I know."

Hoe

She pulled weeds from his ex-wife's garden. Some had started into trees, and she couldn't get to the roots. Bare-handed, she picked up sticks and branches. Baseballs and candy wrappers buried under bushes. Rusty scissors. A barrette. She put the items by the swing. Around her were roses, lilies, bleeding hearts, and many others she would never know by name. There were chives and basil, oregano. He still used the spices in the dishes he prepared. He'd taught her how to make them. She got down on her knees and pulled his lavender by accident. She thought it was dead, but it wasn't.

Kin

On the aunt's deck, they congregated, the mom reminding of an album. "Remember," she said. "That one you got for Christmas." The daughter drank, trying to spot the cat. The cat was always missing. The mom said, "That album. With My Ding-A-Ling." "Oh," the daughter said, leaning over the ledge, grabbing her man's arm like crackpot. She held his hand, massaged it. She had a habit of first massaging knuckles, moving to his fingers, then to the palm. The aunt poured more wine. The night was a quilt of oldness: the daughter back, coming with the pianist, her boyfriend. The mother at the aunt's house, complaining hers was small. This time the mother came with a friend who spoke like a man, saying she liked whiskey. The mother laughed, asked for another sour, confessing to liking it in high school. She went to high school with the aunt and the aunt's husband, and even her ex, who was the aunt's brother and institutionalized. The moon was full, and the famous boyfriend pointed. "It's grand," he said, and his girlfriend lifted her glass to him, then turned around, toasting. They walked around the yard, calling for the cat. "Kin," they all said, running into branches.

Produce

He rushes from booth to booth, vendor to tomato vendor, as if the fruit and veggies will rot and dent before he gets there. When they first went together, he strolled casually, gripping her fingers. But as things rolled along, he sped, getting only what he wanted. Now she strolls to other places, taking in the people and the produce, the potted plants, the children on corners playing violin and tuba. One man, who she learned was named Bandola, played a banjo and sang like Jimi Hendrix. Toddlers used to dance around him. She looks at soap made out of goats' milk, then finds her man standing in a line to purchase green beans. "Get everything?" she says. They walk to his car, placing his bags in the trunk like newborns. In the car, she touches his shoulder. "That Bandola guy, where is he?" "Who?" he says. She moves her hand to his thigh, closer to where it eventually calms him. There is a loud crash, and they look up at the destruction, two cars into one another, fighting for a lane in the intersecting one way.

Log

He followed a schedule, ran in a club. He studied his training and his diet, figuring equations, drinking PowerAid and Gel, comparing that to a banana. She logged the details of her running in a journal: how the air felt on her skin, green or gray, silent, if she'd run through rain or sleet or snow, or gotten heatstroke. He ran miles, timing each of them, getting ready for the Boston. She talked about Chicago, where she crossed the finish vomiting and walking, people cheering, saying, yes you can. She talked about endorphins. He said he didn't get them. They both wore Nikes and drank vodka. They had a mutual friend who they'd met at an intersection.

Purple

The lips got darker as the night wore. I watched the host remove his noodles, tipping the pan, the steam rising through his nostrils. He sprinkled it with cheeses, saying, "Protein." The guests belonged to Gold's Gym, where they trained their muscles, lifting. I went from time to time, when I was in town, visiting my partner, sprinting on the treadmill. The host's wife drank H2O, and the host refilled everyone's Merlot. I asked for Diet 7-Up, though it wasn't what I wanted. The redhead asked for a dry martini. The lesbian pair dirty-danced and talked about their wedding. Kisses, their Persian cat. There was one old man who was shirtless, and seven other couples: a pharmacist, a pianist, physician. The host was a director, Puerto Rican. My partner, Greek, composed. There was a writer and an artist, a speech therapist and a man who taught history at the high school. A gay guy, African-American at the college. There were others, some were students. Me, who was I? The host, he put in tango. Some of us sat on chairs, some went into the kitchen. I ate a bread slice, and saw the rest of them, calling the food tasty. People switched and twirled. I said to the host's wife, Groovy, ain't it? My partner tried to dance with me, like it was the bedroom. I stepped back and went to other persons. I watched their mouths like they were family. My partner came back. "Hi," he said. His lips were dark and sloppy, kind of temporary, though he always told me otherwise.

Casino

My stepfather gave me a roll of quarters, telling me to shake it. I said okay, and stepped up to the machines, hearing them ding and hiss like animals. I thought of laundry money gone, remaining in dirty clothes, nectar stuck to my son's collar. The quarters disappeared like anger, and I watched others around collecting chips. I stepped up to my mom and said, I'm done, and my mom looked on, watching her new husband. He smoked and played craps. "He's going to win," she told me. The next year, at his bedside, I put ointment to his lips, even on his tongue when nothing else helped. At first he held onto the bed rails. But after a while, he just wanted to breathe.

Plug

It was the first coffee shop I found there, where I met a man who played guitar. We went out and drank together, and I tried to keep up, sipping. The lights at his place were always out. I wore tall boots and learned to find my way around it. He had a big piano and played nocturnes. He let me play too and I didn't care how bad I sounded. We went there, to that cafe, every morning—just me and the guitar man. He was tall with glasses, always hung-over from tequila. I drank beer when I was with him. He bought my coffee, cold. I gave him rides. I met another pianist, then moved far for a job that was supposed to make me happy. He has dark hair and an accent, two pianos I only touch when he's away. I dust them carefully. Sometimes when he is sleeping with his earplugs, I sit on the bench and press the pedals very slightly. It has been years. It takes hours for me to drive there. Sometimes the old one comes into the café. He says hello to my boyfriend and they shake hands like strangers. Sometimes I go there alone, where I sit and sip. I sit and sip and sit and sip and sit and sip like rocking, on the chairs. They are old and look drunk.

Catch

She sent me pictures of the cake. They had a flaming onion, whisky sours, steak and fried potatoes. They gambled at the Soaring Eagle, losing hundreds and then thousands. "You got married to my mom," I said to him on my end. I got married at the Justice of the Peace, picking up two people, offering to pay them. The first said no thanks and the second said he was too injured. We found another couple who seemed angelic, their voices a team, an echo. "She's a catch," he said, kind of laughing. I heard him on the exhale. He smoked on the back porch that faced a lake, where we'd once gone fishing, catching nothing worth keeping.

Grappa

The hospital was on a hill and I worked there, in the army. My Toyota didn't make it. I bought a ten-speed. It took me an hour to get there. My calves burned on the up, and I had to get off, walking. Soon I biked it no problem, my colleagues passing, beeping in their autos. My mom came, flying over with her friend, a retired midwife from Memphis. I was riding across the lot to my apartment when she drove up in her rental. I was haggard. She was ready to go. We ate Italian, where I had salad and she and the midwife had linguine. Eat up, she told me. Then she ordered grappa. I went with them for the weekend, over the Black Forest, into the Rhine. We stayed at a bed and breakfast. There's so much to see, she told me, driving fast in her Mercedes. She bought fine wine and said I should get out more. I was glad to get out. I worked at a hospital on a hill where wounded soldiers flew in. Some went on. Some died on the way over. We sat in the room. It was a nice bed and breakfast with clean white sheets. We drank bottles. At first I just sampled.

Handbag

He bought me gifts: a copper bracelet, a book on Cyprus history, a crocheted handbag that would hold the book. He also bought a silver ring and a shirt and matching skirt. The skirt was green and black with sequins. When he was gone, my mother came to visit. She stayed at his place with me and we slept on his bed and she hung her clothes up in his closet. But now she's gone and he's back and I wear the skirt and he orders himself a vodka martini while I sip on Diet Pepsi. On the way back to his place his hand scoots. He likes my skirt. He has a big bed, and when my mother came, she said she noticed that, unlike my childhood, I slept very close to the edge.

Bunny

She got orders and flew over distant lands, picked the van up later, taking the train to Ipswich to retrieve it, her boy clinging to her pants leg and his bottle. She drove over the hills, around curves, taking the boy to daycare. He cried and the providers called, saying, "Can you come, please?" So she left work and he welcomed her with upraised arms. No one had ever welcomed her like that. She grabbed him, kissed him. Arrived. She drove her van over hills and around bends. There were lots of rabbits. They ran out onto roads. They did that. Right when she was coming. She didn't see, and then they thumped and did a bump-bump-bump.

Runway

There were flybys where I lived and I was curious about them. Their sounds pounded on the hollow of my ears. I got used to the sound and smell of airplanes, living on the airbase, and got to know the aircraft schedule, timing it like clockwork. When the airplanes flew and landed at odd times, you knew something wasn't normal. At the base in Mississippi, there was a path on the outline of the airfield, where I would go speed walking, pumping my arms with a pair of plastic dumbbells. I noticed each arrival and ascension, each bird on a mission, gathering for young ones. I would take a break, sitting on a bench, chewing on some celery that I'd packed up in the morning. The carriers were clunky, reminding me of my son's toys I always stepped on. In time, we got on one of those C5s and took a ride to England. The seats were made of net, and the loud roar was a resounding headache. It became a war invading on your eardrum. My son was just a toddler. The plane was packed with other airmen getting stationed other places. I changed Alan's dirty diaper, and the aircrew handed out tin boxes that looked rescued from a junkyard. I had a ham sandwich, gave half of it to Alan and I emptied my juice in Alan's bottle, which I knew he was too old for. The base was full of empty buildings, like a bank waiting for a savings. There were no planes on the airfield and I found solace there, thinking of my husband, who used to stay out late, saying his F16 was having problems. He'd been a mechanic, fixing jets. One day in England there was an air show. I went with Alan to the village and got fish and chips and asked for extra catsup. We came back and spread our lawn chairs. Alan covered his little ears. The planes danced like ballerinas, almost colliding, then floating away. A latecomer would join in at the end of the formation, frolicking like a clown. I pulled Alan on my lap. His shirt was full of bison. I heard the planes roar. Then a bang. A fire had started. Raining pieces of an engine. A parachute descended. I got up to see closer.

Plastic Cups

I'd let my hunger ride, knowing that night there was a party.

We went to Stacy's sister's house and handed her the money, giving her our orders. She must've been twenty-five or thirty, and she put her smoke out, dipping it into the ashtray.

While Stacy and I waited, we babysat; Stacy's niece was two, and she showed us her favorite on TV, some sitcom where the cops always won. She pointed to the good guys then said she had to use the potty.

After Stacy's sister came back with the grocery bag, we said thanks and headed. We stuck the two liters in Styrofoam in Stacy's trunk and had a glass beforehand, riding around with our plastic cups, sipping like the drinks were exotic.

By the time we reached the party, the liters were cold and our cups weren't, so she took hers and I took mine and we drank them straight from the bottle.

I sat on a bench. Some people passed a joint and I took a hit. It never did anything to me, but I felt cool sucking on the paper or the pipe, no matter, like I fit in.

The boy who kept dumping me sat with me and said he heard about my problem. I told him to fuck off, I didn't have a problem, and how would he know? He didn't deserve to know. Like he cared about my problem.

I told Stacy I needed to go.

When we got back to her place, her mom was sitting on the sofa. Her mom was crying. Stacy's niece was running around without her clothes on.

Stacy's mom said I should call my mother. My head was spinning and I asked what for. She said I should go home. She said that when she went to get the baby, she found the car running in the garage with the sister in it. She found the baby sleeping. The dryer was still on. Her mom quivered and started to go on longer but stopped and Stacy sat with her and put her arm around her. I wondered if Stacy was sober. She'd drunk all of her cooler.

My mom came, she stumbled, telling me we had to go home. I cried in the car. My mother said sometimes this stuff just happens. She slurred her words, drunker than me.

Their Own

Her mom was always making. There was always a celebration, a wedding or a birthday, anniversary or graduation. Or a funeral. The last was her uncle Ozzie, who'd hanged himself. He had eleven children, and now his wife Viola, the one with the moles on her chin, cried, and her children sort of stood there.

She, this watcher, relative of sorts, stood there too. The pastor had said Ozzie could have church.

She saw the people mingle, Viola crying, who had never cried at the family gatherings, the card parties, Smear and Sheepshead, eating pretzels, popcorn, Cheetos, the old men slamming the cards so hard on the table the children would imitate, playing games of their own.

Her mother always said not to wear big earrings, that her ears would sag like Viola's, so instead of watching Viola cry, she watched the ears. The earrings were blue and silver, almost touched her shoulders, and she tried to imagine the hollowness of earlobes.

She started to sweat and cracked her knuckles. She remembered a time at Ozzie and Viola's, the Christmas tree, gifts for everyone. They'd all exchanged names Thanksgiving, presenting every Christmas. She'd gotten nice socks.

She watched Viola's earrings shine and dangle.

Wagon

After plowing, my father drove the tractor, and my mother and my sister and I sat on the wagon. When he stopped, we got off and collected stones, tossing them on. My hands got dry and callused, and we all got sunburned. Around lunchtime, my dad stopped the tractor, and my mom opened the cooler, and we all ate the sandwiches she'd mustered. We chugged milk. We threw stones onto the wagon, and when it was full, my dad drove us to the pile that had been there for generations. We unpacked. We added to the old pile, ridding ourselves.

Hooked to His Combine

My mother left, my father went to chase her, and I went out to my father's shed and started up his tractors: his John Deere that was hooked up to his combine. Then his truck. It was big and green from the fifties. I started up the mower, the red antique that used to be my grandpa's. The doorless Ford. I revved up the engines.

Party Tray

She did not tell her husband. It was not her husband's baby.

She kept looking out the window, cutting celery, carrots. Mushrooms.

§

The husband said he'd find the man. Maybe he would kill him.

§

The family sat together, watching sitcoms. They took turns petting.

Wishbook

She sits on the carpet, cutting out of catalogs: cribs and pets and houses, a swing set for the yard. People. She cuts out of the Wishbook, making her inventions: Ken and his wife Barbie, their children. She spreads the households on the floor, the cut-out items: furniture and bedspreads, hampers, trampolines and treadmills. She pretends the people can afford things, caring for their children.

She cuts them. She tells them to be positive.

Mustard

Her gear is ready: her camouflage and boots, her hardhat and her kevlar. Toiletries. She fills her canteen. She watches ice cubes liquefy and crumble.

She hears the TV, the news, and she smells something, finds her toddler, the den, everything in mustard. He shoots the bottle.

Biology

He said to his girlfriend, "Let's go shining." He drove further through the country, stopped his car, shining his beam through the woods. He said, "They're slow tonight." He turned up the stereo and sucked her neck, then sucked it more.

The bus ride to school was an hour. She ate an apple, breakfast.

At school, she took off her turtleneck. The teachers had said she was smart.

Garden

She sat outside and waited, smelling all the Spring, hearing his saxophone, sipping.

He came back with his crystal bowl. She took a cherry and put it in his mouth, watched him wrap his lips around it. "Mmm," he said.

She saw his face on the wall.

Freak

He didn't have a car and so she drove him. They used to work together at a place with milkweed and honey. They used to hang out, months before.

She was looking for a new job, a place with rocks and oceans. He sat broke, on a stool. She bought him one and then another.

She looked at him, drinking vodka. She drove him back to his place. He was a pencil. She undressed him. They fell into each other.

Fly Spray

My father trimmed the cow. He leaned over the stanchion. He wore his gray pants. The cow's hooves were bleeding.

My father wanted me to lead her at the coliseum. Those were the rules.

The cow was bellowing. I petted her and she swished her tail, swatting.

Flowers You Find in Shops

She grew up with cows and chicken coops. Starch in bakery items, peach pies. She grew up in failed farms, crops that died and cows that couldn't produce.

She got up every morning. She picked up her books. She cleaned herself and washed her hair and even put on make-up. She handed out assignments. She took her son to school. She tried to eat at least something.

Floss

Her gums were bleeding. She heard slamming. Her son knocked.

"What," she said. The floss broke, so she tore off another piece.

"I have a feeling," he said.

She opened the door, seeing his blue hair.

He'd been talking about Wicca. He quoted Bible passages, asking her to read them.

"Something terrible's happening," he said.

She looked at his black pants with the chains, his shirt with a Leviticus passage, something about God and fish and shrimp.

She brushed her teeth. She scoured till it stung, remembering him as a baby, smelling his powder. He'd laughed.

He walked in, speaking Revelation.

Ferris Wheel

She was with another man. They'd been in Mexico. She'd looked up at the sun. She tried to find solutions.

They would flutter. Touching, swimming, laughing. He would tell her she was a girl. She was a woman.

They sat next to one another on the airplane. It appeared to be going straight.

Laughing Gas

The boy was eleven. The dentist yanked his tooth. The boy's mother carried him home and the boy giggled and fell backwards.

The mother gave him milk and he threw up on her sweater.

She carried him to bed, and wondered how she looked drunk. She put the tooth under his pillow. She went out to the breezeway, sat on the cement and had whiskey. She talked to him, making things up.

They Took Deep Breaths

In a festive mood, they invited friends. Dip, margaritas. Nobody showed. They sat on the sofa, drinking, eating. They took deep breaths. "What's the point," he said. He went and cleaned. "These are great," she said, finishing up. In bed, they faced the ceiling. "What do you expect," he said. She'd slept there even when he was everywhere else.

She said, "Well," and he turned to her, wanting.

Biohazard

They ran together over hilltops and ravines, through this foreign country. They talked about driving to Paris for the weekend, each finding a man.

"We'll never find him," the first one said.

"Probably never," said the second.

After seven miles through the countryside of Landstuhl, they went back to their workplace, where they showered and changed and went back to their solutions.

Entomology

He gave me fudge. I almost sat on it. He said, "That's for you."

I'd asked him out, saying, "What's up, Valentine?"

We went to this place and drank beer and talked. He was in training. My friend had introduced us. She didn't love him back anymore.

We ate pizza and sipped. I'd run marathons, but my last one was a sinker. He studied bugs. He said he lacked confidence.

Bar Scene

The night before, I'd seen him performing, spreading his fingers on the keyboard. I looked at the Band-Aid glowing from his elbow. I asked him what he wanted.

"Sex," he said.

"I'm not a prostitute," I said.

He said, "Oh?"

Wig

I bought a blonde wig while I was away on business. It was straight and long. When I got back to the hotel, I put it on and thought I looked like Kim Chinquee. I dressed up and walked the streets. Nobody knew me. I could sing praises from a hymnal. My hair was blonde. I wore it home.

Plaid

I saw a bald guy like the one I used to know. I was meeting Todd. He put his hands in his pockets, burying his fingers. He tilted his head and scrunched his eyebrows. He stood in line, and looked around.

I touched his back. He smelled like Listerine. "You look great," he said.

We sat then. He had pretty skin, a small and pointed nose. His lips. He kissed my hand.

He asked about Billy, my son. "He's ten now," I said.

Billy walked up with a plastic thing that you attach to your ear to overhear conversations. "Can I get this?" he said.

I said to Billy, "This is Todd." Their smiles matched.

§

Todd's place looked the same. His dog Muppet got up from the plaid that I remembered wrapping around her. She used to drag it. The blanket was worn with holes. She looked like a carpeted stick.

Billy played with Muppet. "I miss my dad," he said.

Todd spoke. He opened the window and I tried to look past him.

Blood Bank

When he called from his hangar, she imagined the news. She'd watched him leaving on the aircraft. "Jacob's potty training," she said. The babysitter'd told her. She worked in the blood bank, collecting units that would hold in a freezer.

"I gotta go," he said.

She heard their toddler. She went to him. She thought of holding him, but the cries stopped and she left the room.

Tournament

Her son was a batter, slid into base. She watched the dirty water run down and told him they should go to the hospital. He asked for something to bite and she gave him a towel. She looked at his bad leg and watched it fizz. She said, "Are you ok?" He nodded. "Ready for another?" she said, pouring more and watching. She felt faint. He got up and laughed, limping.

Playground

He drove with heavy metal. Then a cop creeped from behind. "Were you speeding?" said his mother.

This was a muscled woman, and the boy gave his permit. "You his mother?" the cop said, in, and the mom handed over everything.

The mom's wrists had been in handcuffs. There was a mug shot. She'd seen the men. She'd washed her hands.

"I'm scared," said the boy. He was growing a moustache.

Boy

My husband left to fill the car. He arrived eating a sandwich and wearing black. I breastfed, burped the baby, then asked for the keys so I could get diapers. My husband ended up driving. In line, he held the baby, bouncing him, making him shriek. I held the diapers. The baby turned white, a gray and blue like purple. My husband faced the baby down, patting his back kind of hard.

Zelda

I did maintenance on Zelda. She was a monster with a temper. She did tests. She was new to the lab. Her rep knew how to soothe her. The lab manager had named her. There was an old model, worn and tired, Zeus, and now he sat on the other end, only serving as a backup.

I followed the list in the binder, filling the blanks. I emptied Zelda's waste, fed her, added tips. She was a giant. I had to lean, into her, opening her like surgery. She was the weight of a freezer, a coffin with wheels; she had a lid, you could put things in and take out, and she had an outlet. She was attached to the computer. She took tubes and information. If a patient's level was five-hundred, she'd scream.

Bob raced over. I was reading a book. He started on about history. He was tall and content when talking. He didn't suck up to anyone.

He asked if I wanted to watch Bobbi. She was blonde and infomercial.

The Baby Had One Candle

They invited people from their workplace. The children romped, licking suckers.

The baby's mother unwrapped with help from the children. "They're all for you," she said, talking to her baby. She pulled the string of a clown and it chuckled.

The Baby Slept Through It All

There wasn't a first name yet. She read the lab slip. She cupped the foot to warm it. She got out her lancet and she squeezed. She punctured, squeezed, trying to collect. The baby wasn't bleeding. So she pricked again, getting a new lancet. She grabbed the heel and the baby was frigid.